MW00946608

The 2000th Warrior

by Stewart and Kelly Marriott

One day in an ancient and long forgotten land, brave warriors buried their weapons deep in the earth. They promised to never fight again because their faith in peace was mightier than their fear of war.

That same day the winds of change blew. And that night a child was born. The child was named Yahtoo Aloo. Just before Yahtoo's birth his brave father went out to fight a great and terrible war, never to return.

As Yahtoo grew, he often wondered what happened to his Brave Father. This wondering caused Yahtoo great worry and fear. One morning Yahtoo's Kind Mother sent him to the stream for water. On his way to the stream, Yahtoo felt a strange breeze. "Could these be the winds of change that the village elders had often spoke of?" He thought to himself.

Yahtoo always felt unsafe. There were
no more warriors in his tribe. As he dipped
his bucket into the stream, he feared that his
village would be attacked. With no more
warriors to defend them, who would protect
him and Kind Mother? Just then one of the
village Wild Boys spotted him and cried out,

"Look, Yahtoo is all alone." Afraid, Yahtoo
dropped his bucket and ran.

Yahtoo ran so far and so fast that
he ran out of breath. He sat down
under the Tall Tall Tree to rest.

Soon the Wild Boys found him. They let out Wild Boy war cries as they captured and tied Yahtoo to the base of the Tall Tall Tree. They called him ugly names and smeared mud on his face, then they left him there.

Alone, far from the longhouse, and scared of the dark forest, Yahtoo cried out until he gave up hope that anyone could hear him.

After the sun set in Father Sky, Yahtoo heard his mother's kind voice.

"Yahtoo? Yahtoo?" She said ...
"Over here mother!" he cried with relief.

Back in the longhouse, Kind Mother lovingly cleaned Yahtoo's muddy face. Then she looked into his sad eyes and said,

"Your Brave Father made me promise that I would teach you this simple truth, "Faith is mightier than fear."

As Yahtoo laid in bed that
night he tried to forget all about
the Wild Boys and the mean
things they had done. He restlessly
fell into a deep deep sleep.

The next day Yahtoo tried to be brave. But once again the Wild Boys caught him, tied him to the Tall Tall Tree, and left him there all alone ... The exact same thing happened the very next day.

And the next .... And the next .... And the next

For many days the Wild Boys tied him to the Tall Tall Tree. And each night when his Kind Mother returned from working in the corn fields, she would untie Yahtoo and tell him stories of his Brave Father.

One night Kind Mother gave Yahtoo a special gift. A beautiful armband with a sacred symbol on it, the broken arrow of peace. Kind Mother placed the armband on his tiny arm and he smiled a big brave smile.

"Thank you Mother!" he said.

The next day, like each day before, Yahtoo found himself standing at the base of the Tall Tall Tree, surrounded by the Wild Boys.

Yahtoo wondered what his Brave Father would do, and smiled. He looked UP and jumped, grabbing ahold of the branch above him.

He pulled himself up and followed a squirrel to the top of the Tall Tall Tree. The Wild Boys scrambled to reach him. Then suddenly a white-horned owl swooped down screeching at them, sending the Wild Boys running.

That night Kind Mother came to free Yahtoo. He was gone. Then Yahtoo called down to Kind Mother.

"LOOK UP!"

"There you are my brave son," said Kind Mother, smiling. Yahtoo smiled back at her. "Come down Yahtoo," said Kind Mother. Yahtoo wanted to join her but he couldn't. Up in the Tall Tall Tree he felt safe from his fears and safe from the Wild Boys. So Kind Mother left him there.

Each night Kind Mother returned with food. Yahtoo shared his food with his new friends, Red Tail and White Face.

After working in the corn fields, Kind Mother would sit for hours at the base of the Tall Tall Tree, encouraging Yahtoo to face his fears. But his fears were so many.

On the next full moon the leaves on the Tall Tall Tree began changing color. Yahtoo played hide and seek with his friends. The red leaves made Red Tail hard to find.

Soon the Wild Boys returned. They began shooting arrows and slinging stones up at Yahtoo. But their weapons could not reach Yahtoo. This made Yahtoo feel safe.

Later that day below the Tall Tall Tree
Kind Mother loaded up a basket of berries.
Yahtoo told her all about the Wild Boys
and how he had escaped their arrows and
stones. Kind Mother replied “I’ve brought
you something very special.”

Yahtoo lifted a mysterious object from the basket. "What is it?" Yahtoo asked, "A hawk feather necklace, it was your Brave Father's," Kind Mother said. "lt has been passed down from father to son for generations, for protection." Yahtoo smiled and put on the necklace.

That night Kind Mother offered her greatest prayer to the Creator. She asked Creator to protect her son and help him to embrace his true destiny. She prayed that Yahtoo would honor their ancestors and let go of his fears.

Later that night, Yahtoo felt the winds of change blow cold and hard against his face as they stripped the Tall Tall Tree of its last remaining leaves.

As he slept, Yahtoo dreamed a great and powerful dream. In his dream he stood at the head of a large ceremonial fire, dressed in the warrior hawk costume. All honored him, even the Wild Boys.

Suddenly Yahtoo woke up from his
dream to the sound of war drums, and
saw big black clouds of smoke
in Father Sky. Then he heard Kind Mother's
loud and panicked voice. "Yahtoo Aloo
come down at once!" she said.

Hearing the fear in Kind Mother's voice,
Yahtoo quickly grabbed his father's necklace
and scurried down the Tall Tall Tree with his
little friends just behind him. Yahtoo embraced
Kind Mother. “I will protect you” he
said with a small and fearless voice. "I know
you will my brave son," Kind Mother said.

Yahtoo and Kind Mother hurried off, following the others to their tribe's gathering place at the head of the Serpent Mound.

The chief decided that their bravest sons, who had not buried their weapons years ago like their warrior fathers, would defend their village.

He called out in a loud voice, "Brave sons come forward and form a line from the Serpent's great head to it's coiled tail."

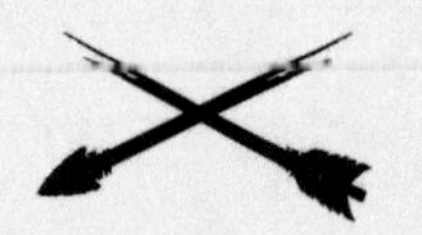

One by one their bravest sons left their mothers and lined up. After the last brave son had joined the line, each was counted and numbered: one thousand nine hundred and ninety nine sons.

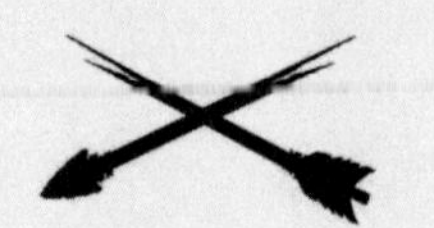

The chief called out: "Do we have a 2,000th warrior?"

Silence ...

The chief called out again, this time much louder than before, "Are there no more brave sons?" Suddenly over the silence of the villagers, they heard a noise high up in the nearby tree. Out of the sky flew a bird-shaped object. It spiraled down from the top of the tree and landed in front of the warrior sons. They stood in awe as the head of the Hawk Costume was lifted up.

Smiling from ear to ear stood Yahtoo, the son of a great warrior. The smallest among them had found his courage and answered the call of their chief. Kind Mother smiled and even the Wild Boys cheered as Yahtoo joined the brave sons.

He was the 2000th warrior.

Yahtoo marched out as one of the 2000 sons. In his brave heart he knew Kind Mothers' words were true, that faith is mightier than fear.

To be continued ...

Acknowledgment:

We would like to acknowledge the following major supporters that helped make this book possible.

Jean Orrico
Dr Bradley Nelson
Margo Hennick
Daryl Hennick
Melissa Frogley
Cory Frogley
Shannon Powell
Jim Powell
Robert Marriott
Danor Gerald
Gerald Auger
Gerald R. Molen
Mark Eisenhut
Les Lobaugh Jr.
Kelly Charles Crab

Our kids: Aisia, Nicolette, Skylar, Addie, Hailey and John Tallen. Thank you for all your suggestions and feedback during all hours of the day and night. Special thanks to our illustrator Sanghamitra Dasgupta, who worked and re-worked each beautifully illustrated page many times until we achieved the final images. Thanks for your creative work and your patience.

A very special thanks to the North American Iroquois Tribes that anciently responded to "The Peace Maker" and Hiawatha's teachings, uniting the five tribes with, "The Great Law of Peace" and burying their weapons for peace. Much of this story has been inspired from the North American Indigenous tribal history's and legends.

We want to thank our mighty Creator for giving us the health, strength, abilities, insight and inspiration to give us this story to tell. We give all the credit and the glory to the All Mighty Creator.

The 2000th Warrior
by Stewart and Kelly Marriott

This book, The 2000th Warrior is the 1st installment of the "Bury Your Inner Weapons 4Peace" global peace consciousness movement.

We are striving to bring increased peace through the promotion of Kindness, Compassion, Tolerance and Respect. Our mission is to influence 100 Million people globally to live with increased inner peace through books, films, music, art, fashion, and social media. For more information visit:

www.buryyourinnerweapons4peace.com

Bury Your Inner Weapons Publishing Company

Made in the USA
San Bernardino, CA
07 April 2019